SING-TAKA-
GDUNG-GDUNG
RAT-TAT-TAT
KIPPITY-BIPP
TAKA-TAK

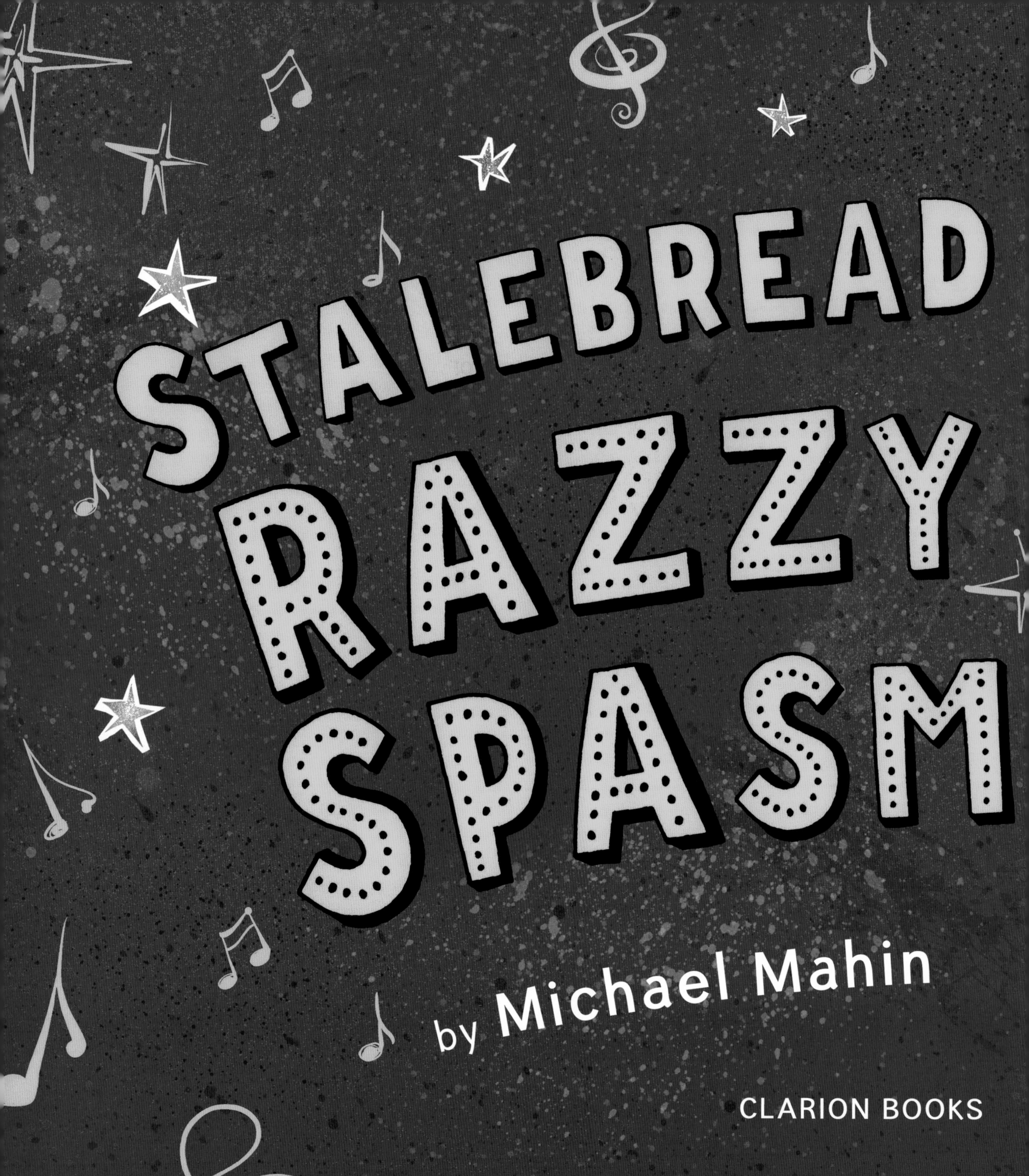
STALEBREAD
RAZZY
SPASM
by Michael Mahin
CLARION BOOKS

Charlie and the Dazzy Band

Illustrated by Don Tate

Houghton Mifflin Harcourt | Boston New York

You've probably heard of jazz music. *Skippity-bippity-be-bop* and all that. And you've probably heard of country: *twang-alang-atwang-alang*. But what about spasm band music? *Sing-taka-taka-scatta-pat-scat*. What do you mean you've never heard of that?

Well, considering that one of the most famous spasm bands of all time was formed by a bunch of kids, I suppose I'd better tell you about it.

15¢ A DOZEN 15¢
MAGAZINE
SPORTING LIFE

In 1895, the New Orleans neighborhood called Storyville was the perfect place to live—if you were an alley cat. It smelled like trash and looked like trouble. But to Stalebread Charlie and Warm Gravy, it was home.

"Get out of here, you rascals!"

Stalebread and Gravy liked to take their food to go. But sometimes they didn't take it fast enough. The boys were hungry, and they had no money to buy food. But coppers don't care *why* you steal, just that you do.

Truth is, Stalebread and Gravy hated stealing almost as much as they hated being hungry. But what else could a couple of homeless kids do?

Stalebread found an old crate and sat down to think.

Across the street, Trombone Bobby bopped a bright beat on his brass horn. One corner over, Guitar Jim wove his bluesy music high into the sky. And somewhere in the middle, Pearly Joe rolled out a rag on a righteous piano.

They say music feeds the soul. Stalebread was starting to wonder if music could feed his belly, too.

"Gravy! We'll start a band. We'll never be hungry again!"

Of all Stalebread's dumb ideas, Gravy thought this one was the best. That is, the dumbest.

"Start a band?" asked Gravy. "We don't even have instruments . . . unless you plan on playing that stovepipe?"

Stalebread picked up the pipe and gave it a quick shine. "Why, this ain't no stovepipe, Gravy . . . It's a megaphone."

"It is?"

"Now I sing, now I sing. Can you hear me when I sing?"
"I can," said Gravy. "I can! But what am I gonna play?"

Gravy joined the alley cats rummaging through the trash, but all he found was a tin can. Stalebread always got the good stuff. He kicked the can hard.

It bonked a beat across the street and stopped at Stalebread's feet.

CORN · SUC

Stalebread picked it up and filled it with pebbles. "Tell me, Gravy, can you play a can?"

Gravy *shookashooka* it and said, "I think I can. I think I can!"

So Stalebread started singin', and Gravy started shakin',
and they both started razzlin', dazzlin', and especially spazzlin'.

But no one liked their music. Not even the alley cats.

"Who ever heard of a stovepipe player and a tin-can man calling themselves a band? You know what you need? A kazoo player . . . like me."

So Cajun jumped in with his comb-made kazoo.

ZIP-ZEE-ZOO,

ZIP-ZEE-ZOO.

"No, no, you're out of key! Wait a second. Listen to me! What you need is a pennywhistler who can stay in tune . . . Here, let me show you."

So Monk joined in with a

SWEET-SOO-SOO,

SWEET-SOO-SOO.

Then came a cigar-box fiddler, and a washboard whiz, and a kid who played spoons like it was nobody's biz.

They were starting to sound like a band.

"Now I sing, now I sing. Can you hear me when I sing?"

"Yes, we can," they all said. "Yes, we can!"

It wasn't long till they earned their first tips. Most of them went like this:

"Get rid of that razzle!"

"Dump that dazzle!"

"And pleeeease, stop that spazzle!"

Nobody had ever heard music like this. And apparently, nobody wanted to.

BLACKSMITH

"Good-for-nothing kids!" cried the copper. "I catch you again, it's off to the Big House!"

The boys scampered to safety. So much for the band. And so much for never being hungry again.

They were back where they'd started, except now there were seven of them to feed instead of two. Things had gone from bad to worse.

"We're hungry, Stalebread," said Warm Gravy. "What are we gonna do?"

"I don't know what we're gonna do, but I can tell you what we're NOT gonna do. We are NOT gonna go to bed hungry."

Stalebread led the boys down to Mac's Restaurant and Saloon. He didn't like stealing, but they were hungry. What were a bunch of homeless kids supposed to do?

The shop master didn't even notice them until Stalebread reached toward the beignets and . . .

. . . started snapping his fingers.

Before the shop master could say a word, the band followed Stalebread's lead and jumped in.

SING-TAKA-TAKA SCATTA-PAT-SCAT

"Now I sing, now I sing. Can you hear me when I sing?"

But the crowd said nothing.

Stalebread swallowed hard. *Maybe everyone is right,* he thought. *Maybe this band* is *a dumb idea. Maybe we* are *just a bunch of silly kids.* Stalebread wanted to run and hide.

But he didn't. Instead, he said, "Louder."

SING-TAKA-TAKA
SCATTA-PAT-SCAT
RAT-TAT
GDUNG-GDUNG
SING-TAKA-TAKA

"Now I sing, now I sing. Can you hear me when I sing?"

Again, the crowd was silent . . . but not for long.

"Yes, we can!" the crowd cheered. "Yes, we can! Play it again! Play it again!"

One song turned into a hundred as Stalebread and the boys played the night away. The crowd loved the razzlin', the dazzlin', and especially the spazzlin'. Most of all, they loved the music.

It bumped and bopped and jumped and stopped, then started all over again. Even the alley cats bounced their bums. That night, the boys filled their hats with coins and their bellies with beignets. But mostly, they filled their souls with music. *Their* music.

It wasn't long till everyone had heard about Stalebread Charlie, Warm Gravy, and the kids that were calling themselves the Razzy Dazzy Spasm Band. Even the most celebrated actress in the world came to hear them once. Their name was famous.

Which is why it got stolen.

Don't worry—the boys and I stole it back.

Author's Note

This is one of the only photos of Stalebread Charlie and the Razzy Dazzy Spasm Band known to exist. Sources disagree on which boy is Stalebread. Which one do you think he is? (from *The Railroad Trainman*, Vol. 16, 1899)

New Orleans is a city like no other. Its rich, multi-ethnic, and multicultural makeup has been the foundation for many distinctive traditions, including many unique musical styles. One of those styles is spasm band music. Often composed of homeless children, spasm bands played a razzy and dazzy blend of blues, folk, gospel, ragtime, brass-band, and dance hall music. Since they couldn't afford store-bought instruments, they made their own out of objects like cigar boxes, stovepipes, wash-boards, and washbasins.

While not much has been written about Stale-bread Charlie, Warm Gravy, and the rest of the Razzy Dazzy Spasm Band, scholars agree that spasm bands like theirs were an important part of the early evolution of American music and what would later be known as jazz.

Jazz is a broad term that refers to a type of music that was invented in the early 1900s by African American musicians who blended the musical traditions of Africa and Europe. By playing the most popular songs of the day, spasm bands like Stalebread's were important because of the way they helped further synthesize, or bring together, the music of these different traditions. Unfortunately, no recordings were ever made of the Razzy Dazzy Spasm Band. Today, the closest thing to spasm band music is what you might hear in a jug band.

What we do know about the real Stalebread Charlie is this: His name was Emile Lacoume and he was born around 1885. He was an orphan, and like many poor children of the time, he found work as a newsboy selling papers on street corners. When he was about ten, he started the Razzy Dazzy Spasm Band, which went on to become one of the most famous spasm bands in New Orleans. Sadly, Stalebread lost his eyesight by the time he was fifteen, but he still became an accomplished musician and continued to play in jazz bands for the rest of his life. He married, had two children, and died in 1946. He is buried at St. Patrick Cemetery No. 1 in New Orleans.

According to historical accounts, the famous actress who came to see them was Sarah Bernhardt. Legend has it that she gave them a silver dollar. That's a twenty-five dollar tip in today's money! It is also true that their name really did get stolen. One day, a group of adult musicians who wanted to capitalize on the reputation Stalebread had built started using the Razzy Dazzy Spasm Band name as their own. When Stalebread and the boys heard about this, they found out where the band was playing and confronted them. When the adults refused to change their name, Stale-bread and the boys started throwing rocks. After that, the imposters quickly agreed!

While Stalebread Charlie, the Razzy Dazzy Spasm Band, and the names of his bandmates are real, this story is a fictionalization. This means that while some things are true, the actual events did not happen exactly like this. I took this approach because there is so little information available about the Razzy Dazzy Spasm Band. Since I did not have very many facts, I tried to be true to the spirit of the band as I saw it. To me, this story contains two universal and important truths: It takes courage to be creative, and creativity (and music) can make the world a better place.

Illustrator's Note

Illustrating positive images of diverse characters in children's books is a niche that I proudly carved for myself early on in my career. I am often sought out by publishers to illustrate manuscripts featuring African Americans. For that reason, when I was first offered the opportunity to illustrate this manuscript, I assumed that Stalebread Charlie and the boys were Black. I was surprised to discover that they were not.

Jazz is a musical genre that influenced every other style of American music. I want to recognize here the role that Black people played in creating jazz and influencing its improvisational style. It's also important, however, to recognize contributions that others, like Stalebread Charlie and Warm Gravy, have made. Jazz is the ultimate American melting pot.

To research this book, I went to New Orleans. As the illustrator—the visual storyteller—I wanted my art to extend the text. In order to accomplish that, I needed to know what Storyville would have looked like, felt like, smelled like—even tasted and sounded like.

I walked many miles through the French Quarter and old New Orleans along Basin and Canal Streets, where Storyville once existed. I visited a jazz bistro and listened to music. I dined on shrimp jambalaya (though I skipped the beignets, preferring a glazed donut any day). I took note of everything as I walked, snapping a lot of photographs along the way. Decaying alleyways hid in the shadows of weather-beaten buildings. Long-forgotten cobblestone streets and streetcar tracks peeked through worn-out pavement. After a while, I stopped to rest on decades-old wooden stairs—as I sat there, I imagined myself as Stalebread Charlie, dusting off a soot-covered stovepipe.

A brick building caught my attention. In its window, historic street lamps were displayed, with information about each lamp. I wandered inside, told the merchant about my book, and asked him questions about the history of the area. He soon pointed me to the Williams Research Center and the Historic New Orleans Collection, just around the corner. I felt like a California miner who'd just struck gold!

At the Williams Research Center I discovered books, archived photos, and illustrations of the French Quarter. Librarians there enthusiastically answered my questions and provided me with more visual references, and then I was on my way. I went back to my hotel room and revised my sketches, adding in some of the historical details.

During the course of my research, I learned that between 1889 and 1913, a small number of Black police officers patrolled the streets of New Orleans. For that reason, I portrayed the police officer in this book as African American. In the end, only a small bit of my visual research actually went into these illustrations. Still, I'm glad that I took the research trip. Visiting old New Orleans made this book-making process all the more rich.

HOW TO ZIP-ZEE-ZOO ON A HOMEMADE KAZOO

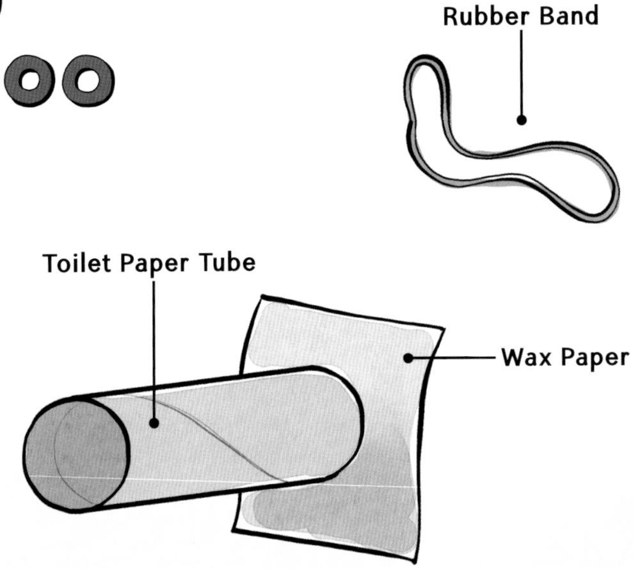

Rubber Band

YOU'LL NEED:

1 toilet paper tube
1 5-inch x 5-inch square of wax paper
1 rubber band

Toilet Paper Tube

Wax Paper

1. Cover one side of the tube with the wax paper.
2. Use the rubber band to secure the wax paper to the end of the tube. You might have to wrap the rubber band a couple of times to get it tight.
3. Put the open end of the tube lightly to your mouth and make a *DOOO* sound.
4. Start a band!

TIPS:

- Don't press the tube too tightly to your mouth, or the sound won't be able to get out.
- It might take a few tries to get the sound just right, so keep playing until you get it.
- The more crinkled the wax paper gets, the less it will buzz.
- Experiment by changing pitches and making different sounds with your mouth.

Visit **www.MichaelMahin.com** for more make-it-yourself music and instrument crafts.

To Dylan, whose music makes
my world a better place —M.M.

To my music-teaching brother, Timothy Tate,
and his razzy dazzy music-making students —D.T.

CLARION BOOKS • 3 Park Avenue, New York, New York 10016 •
Clarion Books is an imprint of Houghton Mifflin Harcourt Publishing Company. • hmhco.com
The illustrations in this book were done in mixed media, digital. • The text was set in Amescote.

LIBRARY OF CONGRESS CATALOGING-IN-PUBLICATION DATA
Names: Mahin, Michael James. | Tate, Don, illustrator. • Title: Stalebread Charlie and The Razzy Dazzy Spasm Band by Michael James Mahin ; illustrated by Don Tate. • Description: Boston ; New York : Clarion Books, Houghton Mifflin Harcourt, • [2018] | Summary: "The fictionalized story about a group of starving, homeless kids in 1890s New Orleans who made their own instruments and started a band that historians now consider an important step in the development of jazz"—Provided by publisher. • Identifiers: LCCN 2016009139 | ISBN 9780547942018 (hardcover) • Subjects: | CYAC: Jazz—Fiction. | Musicians—Fiction. | Bands (Music)—Fiction. Homeless persons—Fiction. | New Orleans (La.)—History—19th century—Fiction.
Classification: LCC PZ7.1.M3464 St 2018 | DDC [E]—dc23
LC record available at https://lccn.loc.gov/2016009139

Manufactured in China | SCP 10 9 8 7 6 5 4 3 2 1 | 4500703428